The Adventures of
Homer the Rabbit

JANE HIGHTOWER

Color Illustrations by Ayin Visitacion

Balboa Press books may be ordered through booksellers or by contacting:

Balboa Press
A Division of Hay House
1663 Liberty Drive
Bloomington, IN 47403
www.balboapress.com
844-682-1282

Because of the dynamic nature of the Internet, any web addresses or links contained in this book may have changed since publication and may no longer be valid. The views expressed in this work are solely those of the author and do not necessarily reflect the views of the publisher, and the publisher hereby disclaims any responsibility for them.

Any people depicted in stock imagery provided by Getty Images are models, and such images are being used for illustrative purposes only. Certain stock imagery © Getty Images.

ISBN: 979-8-7652-2817-3 (sc)
ISBN: 979-8-7652-2816-6 (e)

Print information available on the last page.

Balboa Press rev. date: 05/04/2022

These stories were written many years ago for my two favorite teachers – my daughters Paula Louise Ficara and Kristen Marie Ficara.

Also, special thanks to Caroline Durst.
Her friendship and editing skills are so deeply appreciated.

I had drawn the simple line drawings, but my skill as an artist could never have achieved what Ayin Visitacion did with the full color illustrations. I am awe struck by her talent. She was able to see right into my mind and heart and create beautiful renderings of the characters in the book.

Note to parents: I envisioned this book as a read-aloud book that would both give pleasure and stimulate conversation with your children about important subjects.

Table of Contents

Characters

Homer,	a young Cottontail Rabbit
Mother,	a Cottontail Rabbit
Terrance,	an Eastern Black Racer Snake
Greta,	an American Red Squirrel
Jason,	a Northern Cardinal
Marla,	a North American Beaver
Archie,	a Bombus Bumblebee
Rusty,	a Colorado Chipmunk
Daddy,	Mama, and Pixie – a Human Family
His Majesty,	a big-antlered Stag
Zenith,	a Timber Wolf
Jasmine,	a Timber Wolf
Johnna,	a young Human Girl
Gram,	Johnna's Grandmother
Grace,	a Cottontail Rabbit

Homer Finds a New Home

It was dark and still in the rabbit warren. The midsummer days were very warm. Homer lay quietly against his mother. He was grown up now, almost as big as she. As is the way with rabbits, Homer's mother had a new litter of seven bunny kits. They were all sleeping soundly, snuggled in around Homer and his mother. Homer sighed. He was the only one of the last litter of brothers and sisters still to be home.

"Homer, are you awake?" whispered Mother.

"Yes, Mama," said Homer. "I'm going to find a new home tomorrow."

"Are you sure you want to?" asked Mother.

"You are too crowded here," answered Homer.

"It's never too crowded for you to stay." Mother nuzzled him gently.

"I'm old enough to go."

"Yes, dear, you are. Just don't forget to visit me. I will miss you very much."

"Oh, Mama!" Homer went back to sleep.

The next morning, Homer set off. He pretended to be very brave, but he didn't feel that way.

Soon he had left their part of the forest, and everything looked strange to him. Homer had to remind himself that he wasn't lost, just hunting a home of his own. He found a patch of clover near some rocks and some water gathered in an upturned leaf and had his lunch. Traveling makes a bunny so hungry!

Homer was munching on a particularly big bite of clover when he sensed something slithering and sliding toward him. A black, tapered head popped up right in front of him.

"S-hello, rabbit!"

"Oh! You startled me!" Homer cried out.

"S-I've never seen you before," remarked the snake.

"I've never been here before. I'm Homer, and I'm looking for a new home."

"S-what's wrong with your old one?" asked the snake. Then, afraid he had been rude, he added, "You can call me Terrance. Come see my house." And off he slid.

Homer grabbed one more mouthful of clover and hopped after him.

Terrance led Homer to a pile of rocks and proudly proclaimed, "S-there! The best little home a snake could have. I can slide into the cracks for protection or warm myself on top of the rocks in the sun."

"The on top part sounds nice, but I could never fit inside all those little openings," said Homer.

3

I guess not! I guess not!" chattered a red squirrel from a branch in a nearby tree.

"S-hi there, Greta. This is Homer. He's new around here."

"I know. I also know rabbits can't live in piles of rocks no matter how nice they may be. You would do well to share my tree hole, Homer. Come on up."

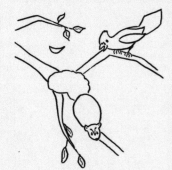

"Gee, thanks," Homer sighed, "but I don't think I can climb trees."

A song with a hint of laughter filled the air. Homer had never heard anything so lovely. It came from a bright red cardinal who flew down and perched on the branch with Greta, and sang.

"I once knew a rabbit who tried to climb a tree,
He tried, and he cried, and he shed a tear,
But he never got up, you see."

"S-that's Jason," Terrance informed Homer. "He's silly, but sings so pretty we don't mind."

"Sing pretty, sing pretty, but my songs are never witty.
Though I try so hard to rhyme,
I really have the toughest time."

4

Homer found himself laughing for the first time that day. Jason's beautiful song with silly words all rolled up together was funny to hear.

"What about your house?" he asked Jason.

"Mine is also in a tree.
Just like Greta's it be,
High up in a tree —
And you can't climb, oh, me!" sang the cardinal.

"What was your old home like?" questioned Greta.

"It was wonderful," Homer sighed. "All dark and dry and warm. But I was getting so big, and Mama had a new litter of kits. Those little bunnies tumble and play all over the place, and it was getting crowded, so I decided I'd better go."

As Homer talked, his new friends realized how much he missed his home. They all remembered how they felt when they first went out on their own. It was fun and exciting but scary and lonely at the same time. Right now, Homer was feeling the lonely part. Tears began to fill his round eyes.

"S-I got an idea! Everyone, follow me," Terrance hissed and he slithered away.

Homer hopped after him, while Jason flew and Greta jumped from tree to tree. A few moments later, they were by the side of a wide creek that gurgled over rocks through the woods.

"S-go and get Marla, will you, Jason? My hiss isn't loud enough to call her."

Jason flew over the water to a mound in the middle of the creek, and then flew back alone. Homer wondered what a Marla was.

Suddenly, a brown head poked up out of the water. A dripping wet body with a large flat tail followed. Homer had never seen a beaver before, and he moved closer to look. Just at that moment, Marla shook the water from her coat.

"Yuck!" cried Homer. The other animals laughed. Marla looked around surprised.

"Oh, I am so sorry, little rabbit. I keep forgetting to look out for you dry animals," crooned Marla.

Homer had never heard a voice so soft, except perhaps his mother's. He didn't care about being all wet; he liked her at once.

"Now, what is all this excitement?" she asked.

"This is Homer," squeaked Greta, "and we are helping him find a new place to live."

"I see," crooned Marla. "Welcome to Timbercreek Forest, Homer." Marla had named the woods. She was clever that way; in fact, all the animals thought she was the smartest of them all.

"Thank you, but I can't squeeze into cracks in rocks, and I can't climb trees," Homer moaned.

"I live in a tree," giggled Marla, "but you must swim to mine."

Homer didn't understand the joke, so Greta explained.

"Marla is a beaver. She lives in trees in a manner of speaking. She cuts trees down with her big teeth and uses them to build her dam. That hill in the middle of the creek is really Marla's house made of tree branches and mud."

 Marla was still giggling at her clever joke when Terrance hissed, "S-we have got to get serious about this problem. Night will fall, and we'll all find ourselves camping out on the edge of the creek with Homer. S-Follow me!"

All the animals followed Terrance again, with Homer bringing up the rear. He was thinking how wonderful his new friends were. They would even stay with him during the night if they couldn't find him shelter!

They soon came to a huge tree with a very big hole down by the roots. It went in one side and came out the other like a tunnel. Terrance stopped there, and the friends gathered around.

Marla the beaver was the first to understand.

"I see why I was needed now," she crooned in her soft voice. "We'll have to do something about the wind and rain whistling through this place. The opening on the sunny side should be the door. Yes, yes, let's see." She began to hunt for branches just the right size for cutting.

Terrance the snake slid this way and that, hissing and issuing instructions. Greta the squirrel began to scrape all the old and rotting leaves out of the tree hollow with her paws. Jason the cardinal sat up in the huge tree singing an encouraging song.

"Homer should be so proud;
His new friends number a crowd.
We're all fixing a beautiful home
He can call his very own.
We'll have a day of work and fix up a house.
He'll not sleep cold; he'll be snug as a mouse."

No one was very impressed with Jason's lyrics, but the thrill of his voice filling the air kept them working gaily. Greta had cleaned out the hollow and was bringing in fresh dry leaves. Homer got the idea and hopped over to help her.

Meanwhile, Marla the beaver was running back and forth to the creek, bringing piles of mud on her flat tail. She would pile branches against the unwanted opening of the tree and pat, pat, pat the mud in to hold them. The hot sun was baking it hard and dry.

The job was big and the animals worked until the sun began to set. The opening was sealed tight against the wind and rain, and the hollow tree was lined with fresh, dry leaves. The animals were all tired and ready to sleep. Marla the beaver rubbed her nose against Homer's and started home to the creek, her tired, flat tail dragging the ground.

Greta the squirrel followed her lead, rubbed Homer's nose, and scampered off into the woods. Even Terrance's hiss sounded tired as he slid from view towards his pile of rocks.

Jason's song became fainter and fainter as he flew back to his nest.

"I'm a tired old bird, my word, my word.
Worked hard all day – didn't want to play.
It was for a new friend, good friend to the end.
It was the best day yet, won't forget, won't forget."

Homer watched them go, and his heart felt very warm. He hopped into his new home and burrowed into the nice dry leaves. Just as he was about to fall asleep, Homer heard a buzzing sound. He looked up and saw a large yellow and black bumblebee hovering in the opening of his tree hollow.

"Hi, neighbor! I'm Archie." Her voice sounded unusually loud for such a little being.

"Hello. I'm Homer, and I'm new here."

"I know, neighbor. Saw you and the gang working while I was buzzing back and forth gathering nectar from flowers. The girls and I make honey out of the flower nectar we gather."

"Where do you live? And isn't Archie a boy's name?" Homer had so many questions.

"It's a nickname and means true and bold. I live in a beehive right above you in this tree. That's why I came to see you. I know where best clover patches are. You're going to be hungry in the morning, and I'll take you there. Good night, neighbor."

Archie buzzed off before Homer could even say thanks. He smiled to himself and snuggled down to sleep.

Homer was to have many opportunities to say thank you and return the kindness of his friends in the next few weeks.

Then one morning, when he was down drinking from the creek, he sensed someone nearby. He looked up and saw a small chipmunk with a lost look on his face.

"Hi, I'm Homer. Are you new here?"

"Yes," came the shy reply. "My name is Rusty, and I've got to find a new home."

Homer grinned broadly.

"You are going to LOVE it here, Rusty." He began to thump his foot on the ground in a loud tattoo. "Newcomer, newcomer!" he called.

A sleek black snake slithered toward them and curled up nearby. A red squirrel chattered down from a tree. A cardinal flew down and sang a friendly song of welcome. A brown beaver pulled out of the water, shook all over everyone, and apologized in a soft, sweet voice.

Rusty smiled.

"Yes, I think I'm going to be happy here."

Strangers in Timbercreek Forest

There was something different in the air. Homer knew it the moment he woke up and looked around his hollow tree home. The morning sun was streaming in through the opening of the hollow and warming his bunny fur. That was the same. That happened every morning. He looked outside. The dew on the grass made it sparkle like diamonds. That was the same, too.

Homer hopped out into the bright morning. The heat of the summer was cooling as early autumn arrived. Some of the leaves were already changing color. That wasn't it. He suddenly knew what was different. It was too quiet. Jason, the bright red cardinal, wasn't there to sing his usual song of greeting. Homer felt uneasy because Jason usually came every morning.

Homer looked up at the beehive high above in his tree. He spotted the bumblebee.

"Morning, Archie. Do you know where Jason is?" he asked.

"No time to chat, neighbor," buzzed Archie. "I've got to go find nectar. I'll give you all the news tonight." Off she flew in a flash of yellow and black. Archie gathered nectar from flowers all around and saw everything that happened in the Timbercreek Forest. Homer looked forward to the news bulletins Archie gave him each evening.

Homer stretched. Then he hopped down the path toward the creek. He and his friends drank there every morning, and he felt sure he would find someone there. He came to the spot where Rusty the chipmunk usually joined Jason and him. Rusty wasn't there. Neither was Jason. Homer kept on going, wondering at the quiet.

As Homer approached the clearing next to the creek, he saw a strange sight. Jason was hiding in a bush, and with him were Greta the red squirrel, Terrance the black snake, and Rusty the chipmunk. Greta usually met them at the creek in the mornings, but Terrance never came out of his rock pile home until the sun had warmed the rocks. Yet there they all were, peeking around the bush at the clearing. Homer hopped up to them.

"Good morning," he said happily.

"Shhh!" they said, not looking around.

Homer looked over their heads at the clearing. His eyes opened in amazement at what he saw. There by the edge of Timbercreek, right near the spot where the friends drank, were two big people and one little one putting up a BIG BRIGHT ORANGE SOMETHING!

"What are they?" whispered Homer.

14

"We're not sure," said Greta. "We think they are people, but none of us has ever seen one."

"What are they making?"

"S-must be a kind of house," hissed Terrance. "I heard one of them call it a tent."

"They make their own house just like Marla," observed Greta.

> "Though Marla is a beaver who works at a feverish pace,
> Compared to these builders, she'd lose the race,"
> sang Jason in his never-ending rhyme.

"S-we'll have to go upstream now to drink," complained Terrance.

"What a bother. It isn't fair," chirped Rusty.

"Will Marla have to move her beaver dam?" Homer asked.

"I don't think so, Homer. It's in the middle of the water," Greta answered him.

The Timbercreek friends quietly moved away to find a place upstream to drink. When they had their fill, they gathered close and continued talking about the strangers.

Suddenly there was a splash, and the friends were drenched in a shower of water.

"Oh, I am so sorry, my dears," crooned Marla's low, gentle voice.

"Well, what a surprise! I can't believe my eyes!
It's Marla, as wet as a beaver can get," sang Jason with a chuckle.

Marla loved to climb out of the creek and shake water on her friends. They always acted surprised, even if they had seen her coming.

"Have you seen our new neighbors?" Marla asked softly.

"Neighbors? They took our watering spot!" cried Rusty.

"We can come here to drink, Rusty," crooned Marla. "Did you see the child? She's beautiful! I heard the big ones call her Pixie." Marla slipped back into the water. The friends thoughtfully watched her go.

During the next few days, each of them crept back to the bush to peek at the people. They listened to them laugh and sing. They watched them build a fire, cook, and eat. Sometimes the people would play in the water; a parent was always with the child. Sometimes they would walk through the woods, and the child would always run ahead.

Once, the people surprised Terrance sunning on a rock. The child picked up a stone and sent it whistling past Terrance's head.

"No!" said the man sternly.

Terrance slid down behind the rock. He was more startled by that one word than by the stone. It was the first stern word he had heard the people speak. Somehow, he knew the man was protecting him.

"That snake is an eastern black racer. He is a friend of the forest. Give him space, Pixie – you don't want to frighten him. He isn't poisonous, but he can bite. Even if he were poisonous, we mustn't throw stones at him. It's important to remember we are the visitors in his home. He sleeps at night like we do and is active during the day, so we will probably see him again. You know, he is really fast, even faster than other racers."

The child said she was sorry, and Terrance accepted the apology by slithering back up on the rock. The child laughed and ran on.

Terrance took great pride in telling his friends that he was an eastern black racer.

"S-I never knew I had a special name before," he boasted, then added, "and I'm NOT going to bite any of them!"

"Well, Marla thinks the people are pretty special, too," said Rusty. "She has been making repairs on her dam for days that aren't even necessary. She is showing off and the people love to watch her. I heard the big one with the deep voice telling how much she does for the stream and the forest by building her dam and house. He said her dam filters the water, and the pond that forms behind the dam gives fish a good place to live, and cutting down some of the trees lets more sunshine into the forest. I wonder how I help."

"Well, I sing them a song at the end of the day.
They whistle along as they work or they play,
They sit by my tree to hear songs that I raise.
They fill me with glee with their words of praise," sang
Jason, puffed up with pride.

It wasn't long before Homer heard the big person with the soft voice talking to the child.

"Look, there is a little chipmunk. He's small; but he is important to the forest, too. He burrows underground, putting air back in the soil. He spreads seeds around so they can grow, and even spreads a fungus that trees need around their roots. Everybody has an important job in nature. One of our jobs is to make sure everyone else is safe and taken care of. Do you think you can help with that?"

The little blond head bobbed up and down eagerly. Homer was happy Rusty had learned how important he was to the forest.

"How about squirrels, Mama? How are they important?" the little one asked.

"Well, one of their biggest jobs is to bury nuts and seeds all over the forest. They dig some up to eat during the winter. But a lot of them stay buried and sprout in the springtime. Squirrels do something else really fun. Look up in that tree there. See the mushrooms hanging from that branch? A squirrel put them there to dry for winter food."

"Can we eat some, Mama?"

"No, that food doesn't belong to us. We can find some

mushrooms though. Come and I'll show you the ones safe to eat. We'll use them at dinner tonight."

That night when Homer snuggled down to bed in the dry leaves that lined his hollow tree, he had a lot to think about. At first, he had been afraid of the newcomers. Now, he was curious to know more. The other friends seemed to be finding good in them, too. He reminded himself to tell Greta how important she is. He also thought about the little one calling the soft-voiced one Mama. He knew what a mama was – he had one, too. Homer drifted off to sleep.

Early the next morning, before the sun rose, Homer awoke. He knew what he was going to do. He scampered down the path to the Timbercreek. He came to the bush and peeked around. All was quiet at the campsite. He crept past the trees at the edge of the clearing and quietly approached the tent. Morning light began to fill the sky.

Suddenly, the child came out of the tent and caught sight of Homer. Homer stood very still. The child knelt, reached out a hand, and said softly, "Hi, little bunny."

 Frightened, Homer turned to run, but his hind paw caught between a tree root and the ground. He felt pain in his hip and in his paw, and he couldn't get loose. The child was coming closer, talking to Homer, but Homer was so scared he couldn't do anything but struggle. The child reached down to Homer.

"Shall I bite or kick her?" Homer wondered.

The child gently slipped one hand under Homer's tummy and freed his paw with the other hand.

"Oh, poor bunny, poor little bunny. Let me help you," the child crooned softly, reminding Homer of gentle Marla's voice and his mother's voice. The child carried Homer into the tent and held him while the man ran firm fingers over Homer's injured leg.

"I think his hip muscle is strained, Pixie. It will be sore a few days, that's all. We can bandage the cut on his paw. By the time the bandage comes loose, his paw will be healed."

"Can we keep him, Daddy?" asked the child.

"He is a wild creature, Pixie, and must be free. It would be a good idea to try and keep him quiet today, though."

 As it turned out, Homer stayed with the child for several days. The carrots that Pixie fed him were a treat. He had never had anything that sweet before. Pixie petted him and they snuggled at night. The father told them that it would be for only a little while, though. The day would come when the family had to leave Timbercreek Forest.

That day did indeed come. The tent was taken down and everything packed away. Mama handed a paper bag to the child.

"Now, sweetheart, I would like you to walk all around our camp site and pick up any trash that is on the ground. Even if you know it isn't ours, put it in the bag. We want to leave this beautiful place cleaner and better than we found it. That's the way it should always be. It's one way we care for Earth."

A big smile broke out on Pixie's face. She had said she wanted to take care of Earth, and now she knew how. She promised herself she would do this everywhere she went. Homer followed her around as she worked. Finally, Pixie gave Homer a hug and a kiss on his head and the people with the big orange tent left the forest.

Homer ran back to his hollow tree and began to pull all the old leaves out of it. When he was finished, he went out to find fresh, clean leaves. He promised himself he would do this more often. He had learned something, too.

Best of all, though, was the friendship of people he had once thought of as strangers and even been afraid of. Homer knew he and his friends would miss the people. What they didn't know was that the family had decided to return to the same spot the next year to camp.

That would be a happy day.

What's the Matter with Homer

Autumn had left Timbercreek Forest, and winter had come. A soft blanket of snow covered the ground. It was a wet snow that stuck to all the tree branches and made the forest look like a crystal fairyland. The air was crisp, but not terribly cold, and everything smelled fresh and clean.

The sun came up and found its way into the opening of Homer's hollow tree home. It warmed one corner of the hollow, and Homer chose that spot for sleeping. He liked being awakened by the warmth of the rising sun on his soft fur. It was his alarm clock, and on cloudy days when there was no sun, he overslept. But Homer is a bunny, so what does it matter?

This morning, though, Homer felt the sun on his back and burrowed deeper down into the dry leaves, trying to ignore it. He didn't want to get up this morning. After a while, he heard the full-throated song of a bird. It was Jason the bright red cardinal who lives in a nearby tree. He sings a good morning song each day to Homer.

"It's a beautiful sunny day.
You need to come out and play.
We'll drink from the creek nice
Where the big-antlered stag broke the ice."

Usually, Jason's silly words and beautiful song all rolled up together made Homer laugh. This morning, he just pushed farther into the leafy bed, irritated. He didn't want to get up. He didn't want to play. And he sure didn't want to listen to Jason's silly songs. He just wanted to be left alone. And, he wanted to cry. Jason waited a moment then flew down into the hollow.

"Homer, what's the matter with you?
The sun is warm; the sky is blue;
Marla will be out today.
Let's go to the creek – there's plenty to do!"

"Oh, all right, Jason," Homer sighed. He pulled himself out of the dry leaves with effort. Jason watched him, his bright red head cocked to one side. Homer had been acting funny for days now. His ears drooped, and he no longer played in the snow. He hadn't laughed at Jason's songs in a week, and Jason had really tried to amuse him with funny verses.

They started off to the creek. Jason flew in slow circles so he could keep an eye on Homer. Homer hopped along, eyes straight ahead, ears down. He just seemed so sad.

"Good morning, Homer. Good morning, Jason! Good morning, sun! Good morning, snow!" chirped a small voice. It was Rusty, the chipmunk, newest and youngest member of the Timbercreek friends.

"Good morning silly young thing.
Come with us to the spring.

26

There we'll drink water blue,
Where the big-antlered deer broke through!" sang Jason.

Rusty ran beside Homer, looking up at him. Homer didn't say a word.

"Homer, what's the matter with you? You've been so sad. Look, the sun is melting the snow on the trees, and icicles are forming. That's your favorite. Oh, please, Homer, look."

Homer stopped hopping and looked around for the first time that morning. The snow glistened in the sun, and a tear glistened in his eye.

"Oh, dear, Homer! What's the matter with you?" Rusty cried out.

"I don't know, little Rusty. I'll be all right," sighed Homer. "Come on. Let's go on to the creek."

When the three friends arrived at the creek, Greta the red squirrel was there before them. She was drinking from the hole the big stag had made in the ice with his hoof. All the smaller animals called the big stag His Majesty. They were shy of him, but not afraid. He knew they respected him, and he cared for them. When he broke through the ice on the creek each morning to drink, he made the hole large enough so it wouldn't freeze over again until night. Often, this was the only place the small animals could find water during the winter freeze.

Food was harder to find, too. Jason would see green spots on his flights through the Timbercreek Forest. He would tell Homer, and they would go back together – Homer, to nibble the winter grass; Jason, to search for seeds. In return, Jason had an invitation to sleep in Homer's hollow during bad weather. Once, during a terrible thunderstorm, he had taken Homer up on the invitation. They tried to sleep but couldn't, so they told each other stories all night. The Timbercreek animals enjoyed their community life, and, many times depended on it. But Homer didn't seem to be enjoying anything right now.

"Hi ya, Greta!" squeaked Rusty.

"Morning, boys," she answered. "Beautiful day."

> "Beautiful day, indeed,
> With the land in brown and white.
> Yet we have all we need,
> Thanks to the stag of might," sang Jason.

"Yes, His Majesty came through for us again," Greta said. "Say, Homer, what's the matter with you? Are you still blue?"

"Mumble, mumble," said Homer, looking at the ground.

> "Homer's still blue.
> Oh, what shall we do?
> Boo hoo hoo," sang Jason.

"Homer, what is it?" Greta asked again.

"I don't know. I can't say. Nothing seems right," Homer said with a sigh.

"Maybe Terrance could help," squeaked Rusty. Terrance, the snake, had found Rusty a hidey-hole under some bushes to live in. In fact, it was Terrance who had known what a nice home the hollow in the tree would make for Homer once it was fixed up. He had a knack for finding just the perfect home for others. Rusty thought Terrance had the answers to everything.

"Terrance is a snake and sleeps when it's cold,
So he won't freeze, for heaven's sake,
but live to be very old," sang Jason.

Yes, but the sun is warm, and he might be out on his rocks," added Greta hopefully. "Jason, you fly over to the beaver dam and get Marla. Rusty and I will go try and wake Terrance. Homer, you stay right here!"

Homer sat alone while his friends sped off on their errands.

"It's nice to be alone," he thought, "but they will be back, and I can't tell them why I'm sad." He tried to drop his ears some more, but they were already on the ground. Homer couldn't have told you how long he sat there, but suddenly he heard Marla the beaver's soft, silky voice.

"Homer," she crooned, "what's the matter with you?"

"Marla – you're dry!" Homer cried. He was used to her shaking water all over him.

"I used my top door and came across the ice. The water is so cold. Now back to you. Where is your old sparkle? The happy way you wiggle your nose?" She rubbed her nose against his. "Come on, tell Marla." Marla's gentle voice and loving ways were too much for Homer.

"Marla, I've got to talk to someone, but I've been afraid everyone would laugh at me." Homer covered his eyes with his paws.

"I sent Jason to join the others at Terrance's rocks. We are all alone, Homer, so you go ahead and tell me," she encouraged him.

I miss my mother," Homer whispered.

"No! That is terrible!"

"I know," admitted Homer. "I'm too old to miss my mother."

"Oh, Homer, that's not what I meant. No one is too old to miss someone they love, especially their mother! When I started building my own dam, I felt homesick. I thought I was being silly, too, but my daddy told me that homesick is the sickest sick there is."

"Oh, no! What shall I do?" cried Homer.

"That's easy," laughed Marla. "No, really," she said when she saw Homer's horrified face. "This sickness is very easy to cure. Scamper right over and visit your mother for a few days! That will fix everything. You'll just see!"

Homer didn't say a word. Sometimes friends don't need to. He rubbed Marla's nose with his and ran off through Timbercreek Forest.

Later that afternoon, Jason, Greta, and Rusty slipped and slid across the ice to Marla's dam. They called down to her, and she poked her head out.

"Where is Homer? Did you find out anything?" asked Greta.

"Homer went to visit his mother for a few days," Marla crooned happily. "He will be fine now and will have a lot to tell you when he gets back." Her head disappeared into the log and mud dam which is her home. The three friends sat and looked at each other.

"So that was it!" said Greta.

> "To be homesick is very bad.
> It makes you lonely, makes you sad."
> The rest of Jason's song was lost as he flew away.

"Come on, Rusty. Let's go to my house and eat some nuts. You can tell me all about your family," Greta suggested, "and I'll tell you about mine."

"I'm awfully glad Homer is going to be all right now," Rusty said.

"Me, too, Rusty, me, too," said Greta. The red squirrel and the tiny chipmunk scampered off happily into the trees.

Meanwhile, Homer had reached his mother's warren. She was outside with several young rabbits. He didn't even have a chance to call out before she ran up to him and began nuzzling him and telling him how happy she was to see him. Homer's heart was filled with joy and his ears stood straight up.

Homer the Rabbit and the Wolf

Winter was over and spring was here. Or so thought Homer, the rabbit. So what could be happening outside? It was cold and windy, and he could hear branches breaking off the trees all around him. The snow was deep – wait, SNOW? But it's spring. Yes, but one final, terrible ice storm had sneaked into Timbercreek Forest, covered the ground, and lay heavy on all the branches.

Suddenly, Homer heard a great groan, a great creek, a loud snapping sound, and the old tree, with the hollow at its base that was Homer's home, broke away from the ground and began to fall. Homer saw a space open up through the roots and ran for it, getting out just in time.

It was still dark, but the storm had moved on, and the bright moon shining on the ice gave enough light for Homer to see a little. He was cold, so cold, and knew he had to find shelter. There was no one around. Most of his friends were pretty scarce during the winter cold and, no doubt, had dug in again with this storm. Where was he to go?

 Homer poked around here and there, wandering farther and farther from where his tree had fallen. He came to a rocky outcropping with an overhang that gave some shelter from the wind. As he crept underneath the rocky overhang, he felt something soft and warm.

"Hello?" Homer whispered. There was no answer. He remembered the blankets the camping family had and thought maybe they had left one behind. So he snuggled up close to the warm blanket and went to sleep.

The sun came up and the wind died down. It was a cold but bright, beautifully sunny day. Zenith, the timber wolf, opened his eyes and felt happy. His stomach was very full, and he had food for his family. He had gotten lost in the storm and had to find shelter, but he knew he would find his way home.

Zenith grew aware of something soft and warm snuggled up against him. At first, he thought it was one of his pups, but he knew that could not be. They were home in the den with their mother. Slowly and carefully, he turned his body to see what was there. It was a rabbit! A rabbit? How could that be? And why did his heart feel so full? It was the same feeling he had when he looked at his pups or their mother.

He nuzzled the rabbit with his nose. There was no response, so he poked at it with his paw. The rabbit opened his eyes and looked up at him, suddenly afraid.

"Who are you, and what are you doing sleeping curled up against me?" asked Zenith.

"I'm Homer, and I lost my home last night in the storm and was so cold. I thought you were a blanket," Homer said with a quiet voice. "I didn't mean any harm. Please don't be mad."

"I'm not mad, pup, just surprised."

"I'm a rabbit, not a pup, and I'm really glad you aren't mad at me. Do you know where we are?"

"Kind of. I lost my way in the storm, too. But I've been around here and can find my way back."

"Back where?"

"Back to my den and family. It's about a two-hour trot that way," Zenith said pointing through the trees with his nose.

"I think that would take me far away from my home and friends, but I don't know what direction they live in. All this snow and ice confuses me. Nothing looks the same."

"Well, I wasn't thinking of taking you with me, but I can't leave you here! Come on." And Zenith started at a fast trot.

"Stop! Wait! You are going too fast!" cried out Homer, hopping as fast as he could after the big wolf. "Where are we going?"

"I know a place where you will be safe until the ice melts and you can figure out how to get home. Come on. I'll slow down."

Homer and Zenith traveled for a long time. Homer was tired, but Zenith seemed never to tire. He was patient with the slow little rabbit. Homer really did remind the big wolf of his own pups. He knew this rabbit was grown up, but it didn't seem to matter. He liked him anyway.

They came to a stream, and Homer said, "I'll bet this is the same stream near where I live. My friends and I drink from it every day."

That time seemed so far away, but Homer knew it had been just a day ago when he had been with his friends. He believed he would never see their stream or his friends again. He wanted to cry but did not want Zenith to see.

"We better drink some water while we are here." There wasn't a break in the ice covering the stream, so Zenith dug a hole in the ground right up against the edge of the stream, and it filled with water. They both drank, Homer staying back until Zenith was finished. He still wasn't sure of the big wolf.

"Come on, pup. We'll cross on the ice here and go up the other side. I know where this place is." Zenith ran across the ice-covered stream and up the rise on the other side.

Homer followed, but halfway up the steep bank, he slipped and fell back onto the ice-covered stream. He broke through the ice into the freezing water below.

Zenith sprang back down onto the ice, using his weight to break through into the stream, and grabbed at Homer with his teeth. He caught him by the skin on Homer's side and lifted him out of the icy water. He gently placed Homer on some rocks by the side of the stream.

38

Homer knew he had fallen on the hip he had injured that last summer because he could feel it hurting again. Zenith realized he had nipped Homer with his teeth while grabbing for him in the water: he could see a cut on Homer's side.

"I've got to get you to the old woman right away," Zenith growled.

"What old woman?" thought Homer, but he was too cold to ask.

Zenith gently took Homer by the skin on the nape of the neck the way he did their pups when he wanted to move them and began a loping trot through the forest. It seemed to Homer to be a long time, but he would sleep and awaken, sleep and awaken, and lost track of time.

Homer felt himself placed gently on the ground, soft and wet from melting snow. They were near a path, and ahead of them was a girl dressed in a warm, red jacket.

"Hey, Johnna!" Zenith called out. It sounded like a whine and bark to the girl, but she recognized the call. She turned around and saw them.

Putting a basket she carried on the ground, she ran to them, threw her arms around Zenith's neck, and cried out "What are you doing here?" Seeing Homer, she added "And what do you have there?"

Zenith told her about their adventures in whines and yips and growls. She seemed to understand and reached down, picked up Homer, and tucked him into her jacket.

"Come with me, you two. We're almost to Gram's house. She will take care of you both. I was just going to be sure she safely got through that terrible ice storm last night. There are so many big trees around that could fall on her house," Johnna said.

"I know just what you mean," thought Homer and snuggled down inside her jacket. He whimpered a little as he arranged his hip to be comfortable.

Soon, they arrived at a small cottage. Homer had never been in this part of the forest and did not know any humans lived here. The door was opened to them, and the most wonderful warmth, delicious smells, and a loving smile greeted them. Zenith trotted in and rubbed up against the old woman who lived there. She ruffled the hair on his head and bent over, taking his face in her hands and looking directly into his eyes. He licked her face. They stood like that for some time, and it seemed to Homer they were silently speaking to each other.

"Now it's your turn, darling Johnna," the old woman said, taking the girl into her arms.

"Careful, Gram! Not too tight!" Johnna cried out.

"Oh, what do you have for me?"

Johnna grinned, opened her jacket, and handed Homer to Gram. She took him in her hands and held him up to her face. "And who are you, little one?"

He wanted to tell her his name was Homer but thought she wouldn't understand.

"So your name is Homer?" she asked with a laugh, and added, "Yes, you think something, and I will understand. I have a way with all forest beings. Let's get you dry and warm and taken care of. Come on, Johnna, help me with little Homer."

An hour later, Homer was warm and dry. Gram had trimmed his fur away from the cut on his side, where Zenith had nipped him getting him out of the icy water, to clean and bandage it. She had rubbed a warm salve that smelled funny on his aching hip. He was on the floor by the fireplace, eating a handful of lettuce and sliced carrots. The carrots reminded him of the little girl who had camped with her family near his house. Johnna was singing, and her song reminded him of Jason the cardinal who sang to him every morning. He began to get homesick again, but this time for his own home and friends.

"I sure am lucky to have friends I love and miss," Homer said, not realizing he had said it out loud.

"You sure are," Zenith answered. "So you understand why I have to go home to my family. But I will come back in a while and take you back to your part of the forest and your friends."

Gram opened the door, bent down to kiss Zenith's nose, received a huge lick across her face, and he was gone. Johnna just kept singing softly, and Homer fell asleep by the fire.

Then one day, there was a scratching on the door. Gram opened it and Zenith came in with another smaller, black wolf.

 "Oh, you brought her!" Gram cried out. "Jasmine, I've so longed to meet you! Zenith has told me about you and what a good mate and mother you are." Gram spoke to her but sat still in her rocker and kept her eyes looking down and her hands in her lap so Jasmine would know she was safe.

Jasmine slowly went over to her, sniffed her, and then gave her a big lick on the face. She did the same to Johnna. Then she came over to Homer and sniffed him. She began to howl, but Homer could swear she was laughing.

After a time, Gram said to Johnna, "Zenith and Jasmine are going to take Homer home now. You'd best go with them and carry him. He would never be able to keep up." Gram said goodbyes all around, spending a little extra time with Homer since she knew they would probably not see each other again.

Johnna tucked him into her basket, with a soft wool blanket. She and the wolves took off down the path and into the woods at a slow trot, which finally ended at Homer's beloved tree lying on the ground. Homer knew his friends were nearby watching.

"It's all right everyone. Come and meet my new friends," he called out. Jason came first. They all knew he could fly away fastest if the wolves weren't friendly.

"Wolves you are and wolves you be,
But this sweet girl is the one who's pretty," Jason sang.

"Did I just see Zenith roll his eyes?" Homer thought, but he felt thrilled hearing Jason's silly, rhyming song again. "Come on, everyone. It's safe. These are my friends, too."

Homer felt as if his heart would burst as he introduced his beloved new friends to his beloved old ones: Terrance the eastern black racer, Greta the red squirrel, Rusty the chipmunk, even Archie the bee was buzzing around, and Marla the beaver… Marla! Where was Marla?

"Jason, would you fly over and get Marla?" Homer asked

"I'm right here," crooned a soft voice, and Marla came out from behind a tree. "You know, these two wolves are great house builders, too." She pointed to Homer's tree lying on the ground. He saw an opening to a fresh den that had been dug under the huge old tree. "They have been here for days preparing your new home," she said.

Johnna went over and reached deep into the den, placing the blanket from her basket in the very back. There were also treats from Gram that each of them would enjoy in the basket. All Homer could do was laugh and cry at the same time; but they were happy tears. It is true – home is where you make it.

Just a last note, so you know. When the weather got warm, and it felt like summer was near, Homer saw another rabbit while going to drink from Timbercreek. He approached slowly so he wouldn't frighten a possible new friend. As he got close, she turned and looked at him with big, round, gentle eyes.

"Hello, my name is Homer," he nervously said.

"I am Grace," she shyly replied.

"Would you like me to show you where the best place to drink is? And I can show you great clover to eat….and introduce you to all my friends…and would, would you like to come to my house? It's real big and really nice." Homer suddenly got quiet, embarrassed that he was talking so very fast and loud.

"I think I would like all of that, Homer," Grace laughed and touched her nose to his.

They heard the beautiful song of a cardinal coming closer.

A Note About Wolves to the Children Who Read this Book

Wolves are often misunderstood. I know you have probably heard stories about Little Red Riding Hood, the Three Little Pigs, and others in which the wolf is shown to be bad. This is not how real wolves behave.

Wolves are very shy of people and stay away from them. A wolf pack is actually a family. There will be a mama and daddy called the alpha wolves. They are wise and usually kind, but all the other wolves know they are in charge. When the wolf family is worried or times are hard, a wolf will often act the clown, getting others to run and play and not be so upset. Members of the family help the mama take care of the cubs, too.

Wolves hunt together when they need food, never for fun. If there are cubs back at home, the hunters will stuff their stomachs. When they return home, the cubs nip at their lips causing them to throw up some of the food for them to eat. Remember in the story when Zenith woke up after the snow storm and his "stomach was very full, and he had food for his family?" Aren't you glad you don't have to get dinner that way?

There aren't many wolves left in the wild in our country, so it is very important for us all to understand them and protect them. You might enjoy looking up the wolf and wolfdog rescue Apex Protection Project (www.apexprotectionproject.org) to learn more about wolves.

I hope you love nature and all the wonderful beings that live on our Earth. I know that, as you grow up, you will find ways to take care of Earth. There are things you can do right now. It is important that each of us does that. Talk with your parents about ideas.

Thank you for reading my stories. My daughters loved them when they were your age and I hope you do too.

With love, *Jane Hightower*

Printed in the United States
by Baker & Taylor Publisher Services